ISBN 978-1-338-20886-3
10 9 8 7 6 5 4 3 2 1   17 18 19 20 21
Printed in China 68
First printing 2017
Book design by Robin Hoffmann

SHOPKINS

FASHION FRENZY

by Sydney Malone

SCHOLASTIC INC.

Lippy Lips is making a movie about Shopville with Dum Mee Mee. But then her phone rings.

It's Strawberry Kiss calling.
"I have big news!" Strawberry
tells Lippy. "Shady Diva is coming
back to town!"

Lippy remembers the last time that Shady Diva came to town. Lippy had shown Shady all of her best styles. She wanted to be Shady Diva's new fashion muse!

But Shady Diva only
had eyes for Toasty Pop.

Shady loved Toasty's look.

"Will you be my muse?" Shady Diva had asked Toasty Pop. "You can travel the world and shine on the cover of every magazine!"

"No thanks," Toasty had told her. "I would rather stay in Shopville."

Lippy was sad Shady Diva didn't choose her to be her fashion muse.
But now Lippy has a second chance.
"I know Shady Diva will pick me this time!" Lippy says.

Lippy goes straight to the Fashion Boutique and waits outside all night. She wants to be the first Shopkin in line when the shop opens!

The next morning, Lippy is up and ready to go!
"Wake up!" Lippy shouts to her friends. "It's almost
opening time!"

Cheeky Chocolate
and Toasty Pop are
still sleepy.
   "This isn't what
I had in mind when
you said we were
going camping,"
Cheeky says.

"Yeah, why are we
getting up so early?"
asks Toasty.

"Shady Diva will be here any minute!" says Lippy. "She's revealing her new hat collection. Aren't you excited?"

Lippy's friends just want to go back to sleep.

Then Shady comes out of the shop.
"Hello, darlings," Shady says. She spots her muse.
"Toasty, is that you?" she asks. "Come in, come in!"

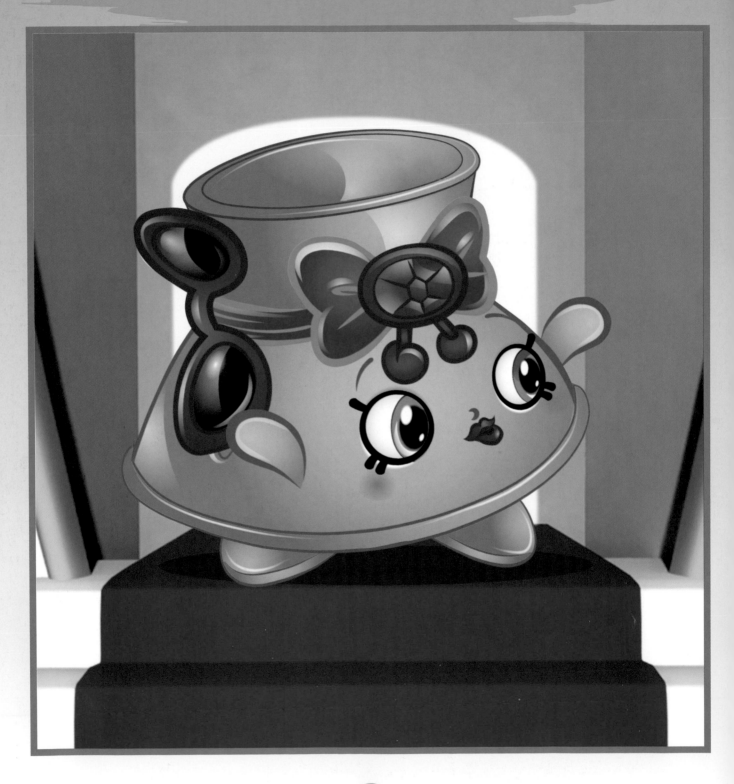

"What about my friends?" asks Toasty. "Can they come, too?"
Lippy hopes Shady invites them all inside!

Shady Diva looks at all of the Shopkins very carefully before answering.
"Fine, fine," Shady finally says. "Everyone can come in!"
The Shopkins follow Shady into her fashion boutique.

"Welcome!" says Shady Diva.
Lippy Lips is so excited to see Shady's new fashions.
What kind of hats has Shady created?

"I'm so glad you're here!" Shady Diva tells Toasty. "I want to show you my latest collection. You were my inspiration!"

"How do I look?" asks Lippy.
She is wearing one of Shady's
new hats.
It looks just like Toasty Pop!

Cheeky models the hat, too.
"Who do I look like?" asks Cheeky.

Now everyone looks just like Toasty!
"Toasties are everywhere!" Toasty cries.
It makes her pop her toast in surprise!

"Have you changed your mind?" Shady Diva
asks Toasty. "Will you travel the world with me
and be my model?"

But Toasty doesn't need a Toasty hat. She's
already the real thing!

"What about Lippy?"
Toasty asks. "She could dress
like me and be your model!"
    Lippy gasps. Could this
be her big chance?
    "Hmm," says Shady.
"I don't think so."

Then Kooky comes in. She found a new hat to model, too. Shady Diva loves Kooky's look!

It looks like Shady Diva picks Kooky to be
her new muse.
"You have got to be kidding me!" Lippy cries.
She can't believe she wasn't chosen again.

"It's okay, Lippy," says Toasty Pop. "If you were Shady's model, you would have to leave Shopville. We would miss you too much!"

"Maybe you're right," says Lippy. "I would never want to leave my friends! I guess Shopville is where I belong after all."